BEHIND THE SCENES AT A MUSIC VIDEO

Melissa Firth

Cavendish
Square

New York

Published in 2015 by Cavendish Square Publishing, LLC
243 5th Avenue, Suite 136, New York, NY 10016

Copyright © 2015 by Cavendish Square Publishing, LLC

First Edition

Website: cavendishsq.com

This publication represents the opinions and views of the author based on his or her personal experience, knowledge, and research. The information in this book serves as a general guide only. The author and publisher have used their best efforts in preparing this book and disclaim liability rising directly or indirectly from the use and application of this book.

CPSIA Compliance Information: Batch #WS14CSQ

All websites were available and accurate when this book was sent to press.

Library of Congress Cataloging-in-Publication Data

Firth, Melissa.
Behind the scenes at a music video / by Melissa Firth.
p. cm. — (VIP tours)
Includes index.
ISBN 978-1-62713-028-8 (hardcover) ISBN 978-1-62713-030-1 (ebook)
1. Music videos — Juvenile literature. 2. Music videos — Production and direction — Juvenile literature. 3. Music videos — History and criticism — Juvenile literature. I. Title.
PN1992.8.M87 F57 2015
791.45—d23

Editorial Director: Dean Miller
Art Director: Jeffrey Talbot
Production Manager: Jennifer Ryder-Talbot
Production Editor: David McNamara

Packaged for Cavendish Square Publishing, LLC by BlueAppleWorks Inc.
Managing Editor: Melissa McClellan
Designer: Tibor Choleva
Photo Research: Joshua Avramson, Melissa McClellan
Copy Editor: Janice Dyer

The photographs in this book are used by permission and through the courtesy of: Cover by Kristian Dowling, Getty Images; p. 5 © Rmarmion/Dreamstime.com; p. 6 © Drx/Dreamstime.com; p. 8 Edward B. Marks and Joseph W. Stern/Public Domain; p. 10 © CBS/Photofest; p. 13 © zqvol/Creative Commons; p. 14 © MCA/Universal Home Video/Photofest; p. 16 © Helga Esteb/Shutterstock.com; p. 18 © Maxim Tarasyugin/Dreamstime.com; p. 21 Carsten Reisinger/Shutterstock.com; p. 22 © Marianmocanu/Dreamstime.com; p. 24, 26, 32 © Pavel Losevsky/Dreamstime.com; p. 25 ollyy/Shutterstock.com; p. 32 © withGod/Shutterstock.com; p. 32 insets © Roxana González/Dreamstime.com; p. 34 Featureflash/Shutterstock.com; p. 37 © face to face/Keystone Press; p. 38 © Scott Griessel/Dreamstime.com; p. 38 inset © Nejron/Dreamstime.com; p. 41 © Stanislav Popov/Shutterstock.com

Printed in the United States of America

CONTENTS

INTRODUCTION

ans want their music and they want it now. How do new and established bands reach a worldwide audience? They make music videos! Music videos are everywhere—online and on television. The goal of a music video is to promote a song, but bands also want people to watch the video again and again and show it to others. In this way, bands make new fans, and keep their old fans happy.

Making a music video can be like making a movie. In fact, many famous Hollywood directors got their start making music videos. As with a movie, to make a good music video you need costumes, a set, a cast, the proper lighting, and a director. The people appearing in the video need to rehearse their moves. If there are dancers, a **choreographer** needs to carefully plan out their steps. But most importantly, you need a good song.

In the end, you need to have fun while making a music video. If you're having fun, people will have fun watching you. And with luck, your video will go **viral**!

How are music videos made? Who is involved? How can you become a part of this exciting process? It's time to cover how music videos all come together.

Many musical acts became well known all over the world because of their great music videos.

THE HISTORY OF VIDEO

Music videos are a key part of the music industry. Although the most important part of a video is the song, the special effects, the set, the costumes, and the story told are what make the video unforgettable. A great video can promote an artist locally as well as around the world. A great music video can help an unknown band reach a brand new audience. Music videos are also a good way for movie directors to get experience.

The First Music Videos

The inspiration for today's music videos began in the late 1890s. George Thomas was the first to put photographic images and music together. He photographed people acting out a performance of a song

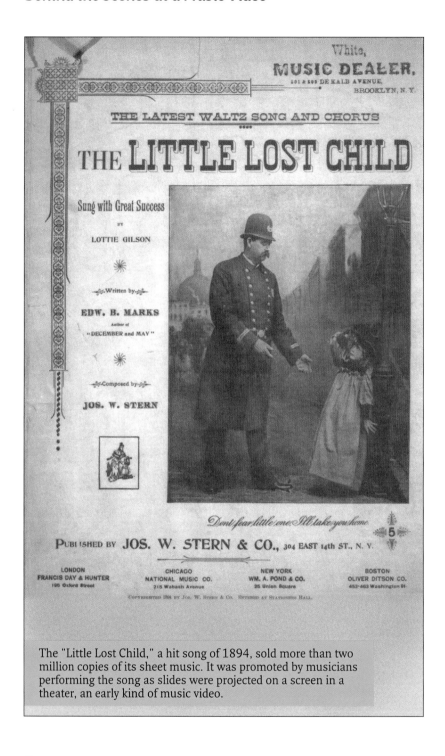

The "Little Lost Child," a hit song of 1894, sold more than two million copies of its sheet music. It was promoted by musicians performing the song as slides were projected on a screen in a theater, an early kind of music video.

called "The Little Lost Child." The images were printed on slides. Each slide was hand-painted to give it color. Musicians in the theater performed the song as the slides were projected onto a screen. This combination of pictures and music was called an illustrated song. At one time, about 10,000 theaters across the United States were showing illustrated songs.

Music on Television

The first regular TV broadcasts began in 1939. At that time, there were only a few hundred televisions in the United States. Over time, more and more people started owning televisions. By 1950, there were about six million televisions in homes across the United States. In the early days, most of the music that was aired on television was for adults.

By the mid-1950s, a huge craze was sweeping the nation: rock and roll. Shows such as *American Bandstand* started showing musical acts that teenagers enjoyed. By 1958, millions of people watched *American Bandstand* every week. The television was becoming an important source for music.

Ed Sullivan introduced the Beatles to America on his TV show in 1964. The British invasion soon took over pop music.

Television helped to introduce the Beatles' music to people in the United States. On February 9, 1964, the Beatles appeared on *The Ed Sullivan Show*. Their performance is thought to be one of the most important moments for rock and roll on television. More than 73 million people watched the Beatles that night. American teenagers went crazy for the band from England. As rock and roll became more popular, television was used to introduce more bands to teenagers. Music on television was no longer just for adults.

Even movies began to shape the future of music videos. The 1964 Beatles' film *A Hard Day's Night* was the inspiration for many music videos. The film's use of slow motion, quick edits, and other film **techniques** helped to blend the movie's images with the music that the Beatles were playing.

During the 1960s and 1970s, TV shows such as *The Monkees* and *The Partridge Family* featured musicians as the stars. Bands also started making videos for their songs. Michael Nesmith, a member of The Monkees, created a half-hour TV show called *Popclips*. *Popclips* showed videos of popular-music artists. In 1980, he sold the show to a company called Warner Amex. The company used the *Popclips* idea to create the Music Television Network (MTV).

The Start of MTV

On August 1, 1981, at 12:01 a.m., MTV became the first music-based TV channel. MTV aired back-to-back music videos. The first video to air was the Buggles' "Video Killed the Radio Star." Within a few months, over two million people were watching

MTV. In two years, more than ten million people were watching.

Soon other TV stations started showing music videos as well. In 1983, the Country Music Television Network (CMT) began showing music videos for country-music fans. Video Hits 1 (VH1) was started by the owners of MTV in 1985. VH1 was created for adult music lovers. In 1995, the Great American Country network (GAC) started showing music videos, too. Between 1992 and 2004, MTV launched music video TV stations around the world to show videos made in each local area.

Today's Music Videos

By the mid-2000s, the times had changed. MTV had mostly stopped showing music videos. Instead,

INSIDER INFO

Over time, people began to recognize the importance of the director in creating a unique vision and style for the videos they worked on. In 1992, MTV started listing the directors of the videos along with the artist and song **credits**.

Lady Antebellum is one of the many popular bands whose videos are shown on country-music TV networks and websites.

fans were watching videos on the Internet. Today, many websites show music videos. Bands and artists often become successful based only on videos that they have posted online.

Music videos have become more interesting and entertaining over time. Special effects are common in music videos today. As film and sound technologies become more advanced, so do music videos. Some of the same special effects that are used in movies are also used to make music videos.

Michael Jackson's "Thriller" is 14 minutes long and plays like a movie. It has been voted the most influential pop-music video of all time.

Music Videos and Movies

In 1983, Michael Jackson's "Thriller" video pushed music videos to a new level. "Thriller" cost about $800,000 to make. It was more like a short movie. The video featured elaborate costumes, makeup, and special effects. At first, MTV was not going to air the video. They thought that the 14-minute video was too long. However, Jackson's record company convinced MTV to show the video. Soon, "Thriller" became the most popular video on MTV.

The album *Thriller* sold more than 800,000 copies in one week. In the decades since the release of *Thriller*, record companies and musical acts have used music videos to promote albums and songs. Creating an excellent video has become almost as important as writing a hit song.

INSIDER INFO

Michael Jackson and his sister Janet Jackson hold the record for the most expensive video ever made. In 1995, it cost about $7,000,000 to make their video for the song "Scream." Lighting cost $175,000, and a computer-generated spaceship cost $65,000. They spent more than $10,000 a day just on makeup! Today, budgets for music videos are often much less than they were in the 1990s. Free video-making tools on the Web make it easy for artists to create a video. The hard part is coming up with an original and creative idea.

Bruno Mars won Best Male Video for "Locked Out of Heaven" at the 2013 MTV awards.

2
MAKING A MUSIC VIDEO

Making a music video is an involved process. There's a significant list of things to do before even a second of video is shot. A budget must be set, and that will determine how the shoot will proceed and the size and experience of the crew.

The Budget

The cost for making a music video can range from a few thousand dollars to hundreds of thousands of dollars for a major artist or band. Today, many artists who are starting out do their own videos without support from a record company. Others may have a contract with a record company. Many record companies will pay to make a video but deduct the cost of making the video from the artist's

Big-budget videos use many technicians and lots of equipment to achieve special effects.

or band's earnings. The number of locations and the size of the crew are based on how much money will be spent on a video. A big-budget music video can involve dozens of crew members and sophisticated special effects.

Types of Videos

There are two basic types of music videos: **performance video** and **concept video**. The performance video shows the artist(s) performing the song. The concept video uses images and story lines that may or may not be related to the song.

Many videos combine elements of both the concept video and the performance video. The idea for a video can come from the artist, the record company, or the video's director. Many directors develop ideas for a video by just listening to the song. The director then writes a **treatment**. A treatment is a written plan for the video. It is used to give the artist an idea of how the director would like the video to look. It includes descriptions of all the visuals that will be in the video, tying them to the song. Sometimes a band will ask several directors to submit treatments for one song. The record company or the artist then chooses the treatment that they like best.

INSIDER INFO

Concept videos often don't have anything to do with the lyrics of the song. The director tries to capture the mood of the song, rather than telling the story directly. In fact, the more stylish and eye-catching the video is, the more popular it often is.

Picking the Crew

Having the right crew can make or break a music video. The crew is responsible for building and lighting the set, doing the artist's makeup, filming the video, and much more. Usually, the treatment that the record company and artist agree on determines what will be done in the music video. However, the crew's decisions, skills, and input on the project are very important and add to the success of the video.

Before Shooting

After the treatment is approved, the planning begins. First, a **storyboard** is made. The storyboard is a set of drawings of each scene in the video. The director often works with an artist whose job is just to draw storyboards. The board shows what the director wants the video to look like. The director follows it as a guide when the video is filmed.

Once the look and feel of the video is decided, the location for filming the video must be chosen. A **location manager** finds a suitable place for

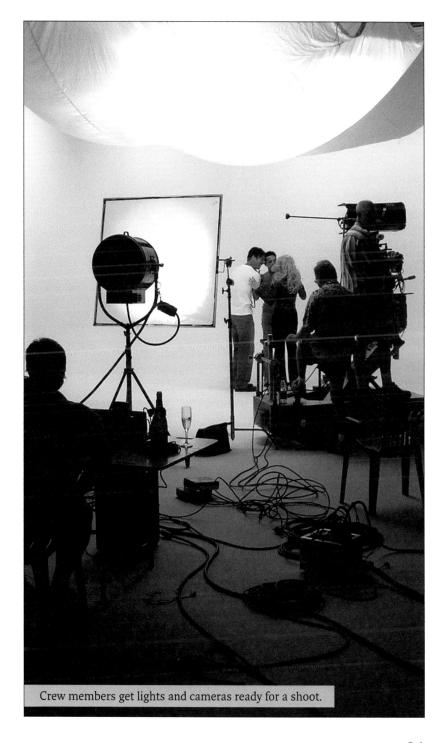

Crew members get lights and cameras ready for a shoot.

When a music video is filmed outside the studio, a **permit** from the city may be needed.

shooting the video. When the director approves the location, the location manager may need to get permission from residents, businesses, and police in the area to film there. Sometimes, special permits to shoot a video are needed. The location manager is responsible for getting these permits by the time shooting begins.

The **producer** of the video has many jobs. The producer helps to schedule the shoot, makes sure expenses don't go over the budget, and oversees the hiring of the crew and performers. A casting agent is often used to hire performers that may be needed in the video. The director can approve or reject any casting decisions.

Before the day of the shoot, the director decides on the different camera angles that will be used in the video. The director may also work closely with a **director of photography (DP)**. The DP chooses the cameras and film to be used in the video. The DP also makes sure that the lighting and the camera movement are right. Sometimes, the DP operates a camera, too. However, in larger video productions, a camera operator is hired to do that.

Production

On the day of the shoot, many people work to make sure that everything goes as planned. Often there is an assistant director who keeps the cast and crew on schedule. **Lighting technicians** set up the lights used in the video. **Sound technicians** are in charge of the playback. The playback is the song the artist sings along to while the video is being filmed.

In videos that use special effects, such as fog, a visual-effects coordinator may be used. The visual-

A director checks the footage right after the video shoot to make sure everything was done right.

effects coordinator makes sure that all special effects happen as the director instructs. Many other people may work on a big-budget music-video set, including a **key craft**, who is responsible for making sure there is enough food for the cast and crew to eat.

Editing

After the video is filmed, it must be edited. This stage is called postproduction. The **editor** works with the director to find the best shots to use. The editor sorts through hours of film to put each scene together as the director wants. If computer effects are needed, computer-graphics artists work their magic during postproduction to create the right effects.

At every stage, the director and the producer are busy making sure that everything goes as planned. Once the video is finished, it is sent to the record company for approval. Then, it is ready to be aired online or on television stations.

Graphic artists use computers to add special effects like these during postproduction of a video.

Music-video directors make sure the right atmosphere is created—like the artificial snow at this shoot.

BEHIND THE SCENES AS A DIRECTOR

Music-video directors often call what they do "musical storytelling." Their goal is to make a memorable, exciting video. Sometimes directors work with the artist to create the idea for the video. Other times they come up with the idea themselves while listening to the song. In either case, having a vivid imagination is an important part of being a good director. But directors also have to be able to bring their ideas into reality.

For a big-budget video, the director may start by talking with the record company and the artist to get an idea of what they have in mind for the video. After getting an idea, the director writes the treatment. All the ideas are written down and sent to the artist and the record company.

INSIDER INFO

Some music-video directors have gone on to direct feature films. Director Spike Jonze started out by directing bands such as Weezer, Beastie Boys, Arcade Fire, Fatboy Slim, and Jay-Z and Kanye West. Now he directs feature films such as *Where the Wild Things Are* and *Her*. He has been nominated for many awards.

Planning the Shoot

After a particular treatment is chosen for a project, the director starts planning the shoot. The director sketches a storyboard, or works with an artist to sketch one. The storyboard gives the director a sense of what the finished video will look like.

If dancing is required in the video, the director hires a choreographer. Next, a location needs to be chosen for the video. If there isn't enough money to hire a location manager, the director may look for some spots. Working in the city is expensive and requires a lot of permits. Another alternative is to find a studio to rent.

Next the director needs to find a director of photography (DP) to work on the project. The director and DP meet to discuss the camera angles that the director wants to have in the video. The DP recommends some cameras and film that could be used to get the look the director wants. The producer and director then hire the rest of the crew: a lighting technician, a sound technician, a camera operator, and an editor. The director also arranges for a caterer to provide meals for the band and crew during the video shoot.

Shooting the Video

The day of the shoot, the director works with the DP and the camera operator to get the cameras set up. The lighting technician and the sound technician set up their equipment. The dancers arrive and rehearse their moves with the choreographer while the rest of the crew finishes getting things ready. The director tells the camera operator to start rolling. The sound technician starts the playback and the dancers begin their performance. If the director, the camera operators, and the DP are pleased with the **takes**, the director moves on to the next scene.

When it's time to film the band, the playback starts. The band sings along and performs the dance moves they learned for the video. Sometimes the team needs to shoot a scene several times to get it right. The director may also want to shoot the band performing their song with instruments. The camera operator often gets some close-up shots of each of the band members.

After Shooting the Video

The director and editor meet at the postproduction facility. The director tells the editor how to order the shots, and they match them up with the music. Sometimes there are problems with the shots. For example, if the color is too bright, the editor needs to fix it. It may take several days to edit the video. Then, the director sends the finished video to the record company or the artist for approval.

A video editor makes final adjustments after the shoot. The editor works closely with the director.

Directing a Low-Budget Music Video

In today's music industry, most music videos get posted online. Many artists do not have a big budget to shoot a video. A director can do many things to keep the budget low. First, the director can hire a small crew where each person can fill many roles. For example, the makeup artist could also look after the wardrobe, or the director could be the DP or editor as well. The director can also look for crew members who want experience and who will work for less money.

31

Artists can make low-budget videos by casting their friends and choosing free locations.

Another way to keep the costs low is to choose free locations to shoot the video that do not need a permit. When planning the shoot, the director can avoid using complicated sets or complex lighting. Using natural lighting is a huge savings. He or she can also do all the casting and use the band or artist's fans as **extras** in the video. The director can even ask the cast of the video to bring their own clothes instead of providing expensive costumes.

Finally, the director can choose to use simple ideas for the video instead of using complicated special effects and props. Being organized by using storyboards and keeping a list of the scenes being shot will help to keep the shoot on budget.

A low-budget music video can be made by only two or three people. It can be filmed in one day using one location, one camera, and basic lighting equipment. Then it would take about three days of editing to be completed. If a low-budget video is shot right, however, it can be just as exciting as a big-budget video.

INSIDER INFO

If there isn't a big budget, the director often uses footage of choreographed dancers and footage of the band performing in the video. The director then edits the footage of the dancers and the band together in a creative way so the video looks great and doesn't cost too much.

Taylor Swift sang her hit song "I Knew You Were Trouble" on a world tour. The video for the song won multiple awards in 2013 including an award for YouTube phenomenon at the inaugural YouTube Music Awards.

BEING PART OF MUSIC VIDEOS

There are many ways to be part of the music-video industry. You might want to direct videos, or you could be part of the crew and look after the lighting, the sound, the costumes, the makeup, or the choreography. The possibilities are endless!

Many schools offer classes in film, fashion, writing, editing, graphic design, and other subjects that would be helpful in creating music videos. Some schools, such as the New York Film Academy, even offer workshops and camps for high-school students. It's important to know the computer programs that are used by professionals. Even if you get a degree in graphic design, you may still need to take computer courses from time to time to keep up with new programs and technology.

INSIDER INFO

In November 2013, Pharrell Williams created the world's first 24-hour interactive music video. He used his song "Happy" from the movie *Despicable Me 2*. The video shows the artist, his famous friends, and regular people dancing to the song—over and over and over again for 24 hours. Four hundred people perform in the video. Pharrell himself performs the song 24 times during the video. Fans can click on a particular time on an interactive clock and watch some of each and any performance.

Many people started their music-video careers by helping out at video- or film-production companies after school or during the summer. Offer to help local production companies in any way that you can. Even if you are just running errands, you will be able to get a feel for the industry and see the kinds of jobs there are in video production. You may also meet people who will know of an opportunity for a better job in the business. If you keep your eyes open and are willing to learn, you could find the job of your dreams.

Pharrell Williams turned his song "Happy"
into the first 24-hour interactive music video.

If you have access to a camera, you and your friends can start making your own music videos right now.

Planning Your Career

You can start planning for your career in music videos now. It's never too early to start getting experience. Help out with school plays. High-school drama clubs almost always need people to help out. It might not involve video, but working with the lighting, sound, makeup, or costumes in a school play can be a valuable experience.

If you are interested in video production, check to see if your local TV stations offer tours. They may not make music videos there, but they use the same type of equipment that is used for making music videos. You could get a look at the studio and become familiar with the equipment. Learn as much as you can and don't be afraid to ask questions. You can also find information about film techniques and video production in books and magazines, and on videos and the Internet.

Make Your Own Videos

Want to make your own video? If you have access to a camera, practice making videos at home.

First, find a song that you would like to use to make a video. Listen to the song a few times. Use your imagination to develop a storyboard. Then start planning the shoot. Ask your friends and family to be part of the video. Choose a location for your video, such as a park or your backyard. Experiment with lighting and props to get different effects. Make sure you have a recording of the song that you can play while filming the video. Finally, borrow a video camera and start shooting. Be creative! You can make a great-looking video with very little money. When you're done, you can post your video online.

You might be able to get help making videos from your school. Check to see if your school has an audio/visual club. Some schools even have video-

INSIDER INFO

In 2013, Canadian astronaut Chris Hadfield filmed the first music video ever made in space. He sang and filmed David Bowie's hit "Space Oddity" while floating in zero gravity. By March 2014, the music video had over 21 million hits.

Some schools offer video-editing classes with teachers who have experience in the field.

production equipment. If you use a digital video recorder, there are computer programs that you can use to edit your video. Start by looking at all the takes and choosing your favorite one for each shot. Make sure to add the audio to the film.

Every little bit of practice or experimentation will increase your experience making music videos. This will improve your odds of getting a job in the music-video industry. Keep pushing and you might end up making music videos for a living!

NEW WORDS

choreographer: the person who arranges dance steps and movements for a show

concept video: a kind of video that has images or a story that may or may not be directly related to the song featured in the video

credits: a list of people who were part of making a video or movie

director of photography (DP): the person who chooses the camera movements and makes sure the lighting is right for filming

editor: the person that uses computer software to evaluate the footage recorded and arrange it into the final music video

extras: people who are hired to be in the background of a video or movie

key craft: the person who looks after food for the cast and crew

lighting technician: the person who sets up and controls the lighting on a set

42

location manager: the person who finds places where a video can be shot

performance video: a kind of video that has an artist or band performing a song

permit: a written statement giving permission for something

producer: the person in charge of schedules, the budget, and the hiring of the crew for a video or movie

sound technician: the person who sets up and controls the sound on a set

storyboard: a set of drawings that shows what the scenes in a filmed production will look like

take: a scene or sequence from recorded footage

techniques: methods or ways of doing something that require skill

treatment: a written plan for a video

viral: a video or image that quickly goes from one Internet user to another

FURTHER INFORMATION

Books

Lanier, Troy. *Filmmaking for Teens: Pulling Off Your Shorts*. Studio City, CA: Michael Wiese Productions, 2010.

Nichols, Kaitlyn. *Make Your Own Music Video*. New York, NY: Klutz, 2010.

Richards, Andrea. *Girl Director: A How-to Guide for the First-Time, Flat-Broke Film and Video Maker*. New York, NY: Ten Speed Press, 2005.

Organizations

Association for Independent Video & Filmmakers

www.aivf.org

PO Box 391620

Cambridge, MA 02139

877-513-7400

Music Video Production Association

www.mvpa.com

201 N. Occidental Street, Building 7, Unit B

Hollywood, California 90026

Websites

Music Video Wire

www.mvwire.com

Provides interviews with music-video directors and information about making music videos.

Videomaker

www.videomaker.com

Includes resources and techniques for making a video, plus forums on different topics.

INDEX

Music Television
Network (MTV), 11,
12, 14, 15, 16

performance video,
18, 19
permits, 22, 28
playback, 23, 29, 30
Popclips, 11
postproduction, 24,
25, 30
producer, 22, 25, 29

rock and roll, 9, 10

shoot, 17, 21, 22, 23,
24, 26, 28, 29, 30,
31, 32, 33, 40
sound technician(s),
23, 29
special effects, 7, 13, 14,
18, 23, 24, **25**, 33
storyboard, 20, 28,
33, 40

techniques, 11, 39
television, 4, 9, 10, 11,
12, 25
Thomas, George, 7
treatment, 19, 20,
27, 28

viral, 5

Williams, Pharrell,
36, **37**

ABOUT THE AUTHOR

Melissa Firth is a Production Stage Manager for a New York theater. A native of East Sussex, United Kingdom, Melissa relocated to the States to study theater. She has worked on countless plays and musicals, and is grateful for the opportunity to work in a career she loves. Melissa lives on Long Island with her husband, two daughters, and their dog, Oso.